W9-CAW-600

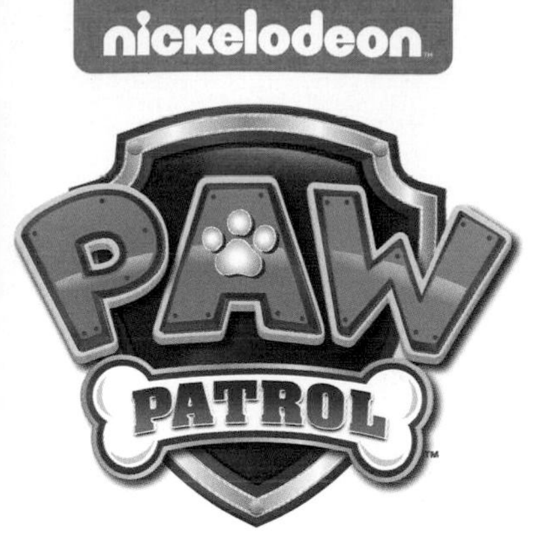

Marshall to the Rescue!

Based on the episode "Pup Pup Goose" by Ursula Ziegler-Sullivan

Illustrated by MJ Illustrations

A GOLDEN BOOK • NEW YORK

randomhousekids.com

ISBN 978-1-101-93847-8

Printed in the United States of America

10 9 8 7 6 5 4 3 2

It was an exciting day at the Lookout. A flock of geese was flying south for the winter, and the birds were going to stop at the Lookout for a rest. To welcome them, Rocky had built a big nest, and Rubble used his shovel to fill it with yummy bread.

Marshall ran over. He was so excited, he accidentally tumbled into the nest. "The geese are coming!" he shouted.

The rest of the team came down from the Lookout to greet the flock, too.

The geese landed and immediately started pecking at the bread. One tired goose happily settled into the nest to relax.

"He likes your nest," Ryder said, patting Rocky.

But a baby goose wandered away from the rest of the flock. He waddled into a blue bucket—and rolled down a hill!

"I'll get him!" Marshall announced, racing after the bucket. As he ran down the hill, his feet got tangled. Marshall *and* the goose ended up bouncing down the hill!

When they reached the bottom, they were both a little dizzy.

"Are you okay, fuzzy little guy?" Marshall asked.

"Cheep! Cheep!" the goose replied with a nod.

"Hey!" Marshall exclaimed. "Fuzzy is a great name for you!"

Marshall took Fuzzy back to the Lookout, where he introduced him to the rest of the PAW Patrol. The little goose liked all the pups, but Marshall was definitely his favorite.

Skye chuckled. "Marshall, it looks like you have a new BGFF—Best Goose Friend Forever!"

For the rest of the day, the two friends did everything together. When Marshall tripped over his dog bowl, so did Fuzzy.

When Marshall washed his fire truck, Fuzzy polished the window with his feathers . . .

until Marshall accidentally "washed" him with his hose!

"Sorry, Fuzzy," said Marshall.

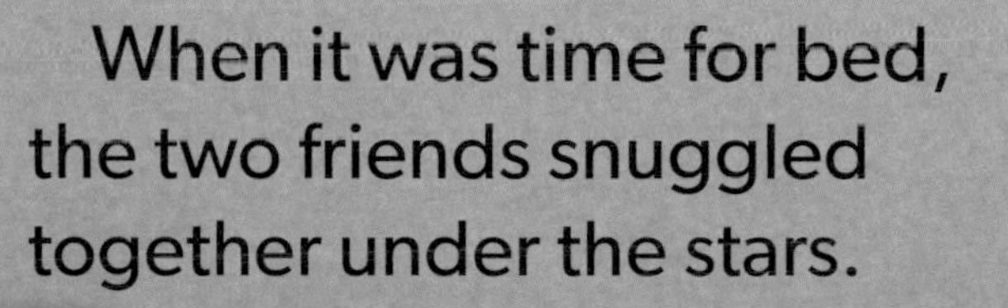

When it was time for bed, the two friends snuggled together under the stars.

Just before dawn, Fuzzy woke up. He was hungry, so he wandered off, looking for food.

Marshall woke up later and couldn't find the little goose. He was worried, so he went to Ryder.

Ryder called the PAW Patrol to the Lookout.

"Our geese friends have to fly south for the winter," he explained. "But they're missing one little goose. If we don't find Fuzzy fast, they'll have to leave without him! Chase, I need you to call Fuzzy with your megaphone. Marshall, Fuzzy would follow you anywhere—I need you to help look for him, too!"

Outside the Lookout, Chase called to the lost goose. Marshall sniffed the ground in search of clues. He found one of Fuzzy's feathers! Ryder picked it up, and Chase took a whiff.

"ACHOO!" Chase sneezed. "Sorry—I'm a little allergic to feathers." He took a few more sniffs, sneezed, and announced, "He went this way!"

Ryder, Chase, and Marshall jumped into their vehicles and followed Fuzzy's trail into Adventure Bay.

The team searched all around town, but they couldn't find Fuzzy. Suddenly, Marshall heard some chirping high above them. Fuzzy was on the roof of the train station! He had a piece of bread in his beak, and some seagulls were trying to take it.

"Pick on someone your own size!" Chase shouted at the bullying birds.

"Fuzzy, fly down here!" Marshall called.

But Fuzzy couldn't fly down.

"A plastic soda-can ring is wrapped around his wing," Ryder said. "Marshall, quick! Use your ladder to help get Fuzzy down!"

Marshall was on it!

Marshall extended the ladder on his fire truck, which scared away the seagulls. As he started to climb up, Fuzzy tried to run to him—and fell! Marshall quickly held out his fire helmet and caught the little goose.

"Sweet catch, Marshall!" Ryder cheered.

Back on the ground, Ryder carefully removed the plastic ring from Fuzzy. The little bird was free. He could fly again!

The PAW Patrol raced back to the Lookout. They had to get there before Fuzzy's flock flew away.

But they were too late—the geese had just left! Fuzzy would have to flap fast to catch up to them.

Fuzzy didn't want to go, and Marshall didn't want him to leave, either.

"A little gosling belongs with his family," Ryder said.

Marshall agreed, and Ryder quickly came up with a plan to return Fuzzy to his flock.

"Let's take to the sky!" Skye exclaimed as her helicopter zoomed into the air, pulling Marshall along in a harness.

"Come on, Fuzzy!" Marshall shouted. "Time to fly with me! Flap! Flap!"

The baby goose wanted to follow Marshall! Fuzzy flapped his wings, rose from the ground, and flew into the air.

Marshall, Skye, and Fuzzy could see the flock in the distance. Fuzzy flew as fast as he could until he finally caught up with his family. He chirped goodbye to Marshall.

"Goodbye, Fuzzy," Marshall called with a teary sniffle. "Have a safe flight, you silly goose!"

Back at the Lookout, the pups played jump rope.

"You guys did an awesome job today," Ryder said.

Marshall missed Fuzzy, but he knew his little friend would visit whenever his family flew overhead. Until then, he had his *paw*some pup pals to keep him company!